DOCTOR·WHO

DECIDE YOUR DESTINY

BBC CHILDREN'S BOOKS
Published by the Penguin Group
Penguin Books Ltd, 80 Strand, London, WC2R 0RL, England
Penguin Group (USA) Inc., 375 Hudson Street, New York, New York 10014, USA
Penguin Books (Australia) Ltd, 250 Camberwell Road, Camberwell, Victoria 3124, Australia.
(A division of Pearson Australia Group Pty Ltd)
Canada, India, New Zealand, South Africa
Published by BBC Children's Books, 2007
This edition produced for The Book People Ltd, Hall Wood Avenue, Haydock, St Helens. WA11 9UL.
Text and design © Children's Character Books, 2007
Written by Colin Brake
10 9 8 7 6 5 4 3 2 1
ISBN-13: 978-1-85613-145-2
ISBN-10: 1-85613-145-9
Printed in Great Britain by Clays Ltd, St Ives plc

DOCTOR · WHO

DECIDE YOUR DESTINY

The Time Crocodile

by Colin Brake

The Time Crocodile

1 | They call it the TARDIS. It's a space/time ship. It can travel anywhere in time and space. From the outside it looks like a sort of shed painted blue but inside it's much, much bigger. Impossibly big!

You're standing inside the ship's control room. It's a massive domed space with a raised platform in the middle, where an odd collection of controls is housed on a many-sided console. A man is on the platform, consulting the screens and some of the numerous read-outs. This is the Doctor, the owner of the time and space machine.

'Are you okay?' asks a concerned voice. This is Martha, the Doctor's companion, a pretty girl in her twenties. She has a kind voice and twinkling eyes. She's from Earth like you, but she's a bit more experienced with this space/time travel business. It is Martha who has been explaining about the Doctor and his TARDIS.

You tell her you're fine and ask her if she is a doctor too. She laughs.

'Not quite. I'm a medical student, which means I will be a doctor one day.' Martha looks at the Doctor and grins as she speaks. 'Right now I'm taking a bit of time off to do a little travelling,' she continues.

'Lots of students do it,' says the Doctor chipping in, 'Only most tend to stick to Earth!'

Feeling more at ease you apologise for wandering into the TARDIS when you found it half-hidden in the trees at the park. The Doctor says sorry again for taking off with you on board and promises to try and get you home, but you want to see how the TARDIS works.

If you ask politely to have a trip in the TARDIS, go to 44. If you keep quiet and wait to see what happens, go to 98.

2 For a moment Professor Morrow stares at you, the raised blaster in his hands. And then, before he can say or do anything, the door slams shut again, cutting him off.

'What did you do?' you ask the Doctor.

'I didn't do anything,' he tells you, as astounded as you are.

'But I did,' comes a new voice. It's the tortoise. He and Martha are hurrying towards you.

'Professor Morrow's totally lost his mind.'

'That's not all he's going to lose,' the Doctor replies. 'We need to get back to the TARDIS. I have to get to the point where the time experiment started.' The Doctor grins wildly. 'Time is of the essence!'

You and Martha spot an electric truck used to take supplies round the zoo. 'Could this help?'

If you get back to the TARDIS on the truck, go to 33. If Professor Morrow finds you, go to 90.

3 You wander out into an area filled with cages and enclosures but you have to admit you are a little bit disappointed at how normal it looks.

'It looks a bit like any other zoo,' you tell the Doctor.

'Do you really think so?' he asks you, frowning.

'Well, it looks like a zoo and smells like a zoo. The only thing missing is...'

You look around, aware that something is wrong with the picture but unable to work out what it is. Then it hits you.

'There's no people. No visitors, no staff.' you comment, 'All a bit boring really.'

'If it's boring out there, try being on this side of the glass!' adds a new voice.

You spin around looking for the source of the voice.

If it has come from a cage to the left, go to 18. If it has come from a cage to the right, go to 79.

4 You go through the door and find yourself in an area filled with animal cages and enclosures. The Doctor is happily looking into each one.

'Interesting zoo, isn't it?' he says as you join him.

'It looks like any other zoo,' you reply, with a shrug.

'Does it?' The Doctor raises a quizzical eyebrow.

He suggests that you and Martha should take another look.

You do as he suggests but it really does look like every zoo you've ever been in. Animal enclosures, brightly coloured signs, litter bins. Everything except an ice cream kiosk.

'Shame, I'd love a 99,' mutters the Doctor when you mention this.

'Wait a minute,' Martha interjects, 'Where are all the people?'

'You want to try being on this side of the glass,' a new voice complains.

If the voice has come from the left, go to 18. If the voice has come from the right, go to 79.

5 You turn around and are delighted to see that Martha is there, giving the Doctor a quick hug. She then comes across to you and gives you a kiss on the cheek too.

'Thank you,' she tells you, with evident relief.

'Where have you been?' you ask.

'Here!' she says, a little annoyed, 'I've been with you all the time but, apparently, invisible. And inaudible!'

'Displaced in time,' explains the Doctor.

'Whatever!' Martha grins, 'At least I'm here to help now.'

'Looks like our young friend here managed to fill in for you,' the Doctor says, 'but we'd better see about getting you home now, I think.'

A little while later you are back inside the TARDIS. The Doctor suggests you might like to launch the TARDIS and points you to a control to pull.

If you pull a lever, go to 70. If you decline, go to 53.

6 Terrific blows are buffering the TARDIS and it is difficult for you to keep your balance. The Doctor skips round the many-sided console and manages to move the lever that you couldn't get to shift.

The Time Crocodile laughs.

'This weird ship of yours is tougher than she looks!' he comments.

'Her pilot's no pushover, either,' the Doctor comments, with a hint of a threat.

'Hey, no offence meant, mate,' the crocodile hurriedly adds, 'I was just making an observation.'

The Doctor concentrates on his instruments. The ride is still rather rough and you're beginning to feel sick.

'Hold on,' announces the Doctor, 'This might be a rough landing.'

Seconds later the TARDIS appears to flip through a complete circle.

You find yourself flung into the air and land poorly, banging your head.

If you pass out, go to 11. If you manage to stay conscious, go to 46.

7 The Time Crocodile comes up to you and you involuntarily back away.

'It's okay, I'm not going to hurt you,' says the crocodile with a sigh.

You apologise and try to stop your heart from racing. It's not easy, standing so close to a three metre long crocodile.

'So how does this work then?' you ask, trying to keep your voice from trembling.

'You need to be touching me,' answers the crocodile. 'Why don't you get on my back?'

You climb onto the crocodile's back and sit down. It's a bit like sitting on a see-saw that's way too small for you. The crocodile's skin is scaly and cold.

'Now I have to concentrate.' The crocodile closes his eyes and begins chanting. And then suddenly everything around you begins to fade. You feel yourself getting dizzy.

If you pass out, go to 11. If you keep conscious, go to 45.

8 | The tortoise leads you along a corridor. You and Martha are fascinated by the odd familiarity of the zoo.

'Just like a zoo back home, isn't it?' Martha comments. You nod in agreement and jump suddenly as an alarm begins to sound.

'This way!' cries the tortoise. But before you can do anything, a sliding security door drops from the ceiling. Martha and the tortoise are trapped on the other side.

'Martha!' you call out but before you try and open the door the Doctor is grabbing you by the hand and pulling you in the opposite direction.

'Stop or I'll shoot,' someone shouts at you. It's a manic-looking man in a white coat holding some kind of weapon.

If the Doctor uses his sonic screwdriver to activate another security door, go to 74. If the Doctor pulls you through the nearest door, go to 13.

The Doctor hurriedly leads you back to the TARDIS.

You are full of questions but the Doctor hushes you.

Once in the TARDIS he rushes to the Console. You try again with your questions.

'What happened to the Time Crocodile?'

The Doctor doesn't look up from the controls.

'Gone.'

'And Martha?'

The Doctor doesn't reply but pulls a lever causing a burst of electrical sparks to fly out of the console. A glowing light appears from which Martha emerges.

'I'm here!' she says, grinning, 'I've been with you all the time but, apparently, invisible.'

'Displaced in time,' adds the Doctor.

'Whatever!' Martha grins.

The Doctor looks at you 'I think we'd better see about getting our young friend home now, don't you?'

He indicates a particular lever on the console. 'Would you like to start us up?'

If you pull a lever, go to 70. If you decline, go to 53.

10 When you reach the Control Centre you find it alive with activity. All the screens are active and there's a massive buzz of electrical equipment.

'It's the same as before,' you say, a little disappointed.

'Not at all,' replies the Doctor.

He points at one of the screens. 'The Professor's trying to generate a time bridge... He's managed to get hold of something that has travelled through time,' he explains.

'I don't understand,' you tell him.

'Anything that travels through time picks up time particles — little bits of the Time Vortex. If you're clever enough — or mad enough — you can use them to create a crude time machine...'

'Is it dangerous?' you ask.

'Extremely,' the Doctor looks very serious. 'We have to shut it down.'

'Doctor!' It's the Time Crocodile. 'I think you should look at this.'

If he sounds frightened, go to 105. If he sounds upset, go to 101.

11 You're not sure where you are. Your head is aching. You open your eyes but at first everything is a blur. Then you hear a familiar voice.

'Here drink this.' It's the Doctor. He hands you a cup of water, which you take and drink straight down. 'Thank you,' you say, feeling a bit better.

'Where am I?' you ask.

The Doctor smiles. 'At the zoo. Forty-eight hours before we first arrived, remember?'

'I was having this weird dream... there was this talking crocodile...' you begin but another voice interrupts you.

'I'm here too,' he rumbles.

Now you see that the Time Crocodile is standing beside the Doctor.

'We're all here,' the Doctor tells you, 'one way or another.'

'What next then?' you ask.

The Doctor grins. 'Let's find the Professor.'

If you arrived in the TARDIS, go to 12. If you travelled by Time Crocodile, go to 10.

The zoo in the past doesn't look any different. It still feels unnaturally quiet and rather sad. Exploring it again it's much clearer that it has fallen on hard times.

The only signs of life are squat white robots with multiple function arm attachments that suddenly appear and start distributing food to the various cages. You ask the Doctor if they are dangerous but he explains that these are just simple maintenance robots.

'So why didn't we see any in the future?' you ask.

'Let's ask one of the inmates.'

The Doctor goes up to the nearest enclosure.

Inside is a giant tortoise — quietly nibbling on a lettuce.

'Hello,' says the Doctor, politely. You get no answer.

If you decide to forget the tortoise and go directly to the Control Centre, go to 10. If you prefer to try and talk to the tortoise again, go to 54.

13 You run into a room full of strange mechanical equipment that is linked by pulsing cables. There is a constant murmur of electrical power. The Doctor examines the device in more detail.

'Oh no...' he utters, with a look of horror on his face. 'Oh this is very bad... Totally amateur.'

The more he looks at it, the more worried he seems to be.

'What exactly is it?' you ask.

The Doctor turns to you with a very serious expression on his face. He almost seems afraid. 'It's a very poor attempt to create a time window. And it's not very stable.'

'Can you shut it down?'

'I don't know but I have to try. And I can't do it from here.'

Another security door begins to open.

If it rises to reveal Martha and the tortoise, go to 66. If it rises to reveal Professor Morrow, go to 2.

The Doctor taps politely on the shell of the tortoise.

'Excuse me,' he asks, trying not to laugh, 'But I wonder if you can help us?'

The tortoise pops his head out.

'How do I know I can trust you?' he asks, suspiciously.

'Please,' you say, 'we just want to know what's going on.'

'You need to talk to Professor Morrow then,' answers the tortoise, tartly. 'Or the Time Crocodile.'

'The what?' you ask.

'The Time Croc is the Professor's pet — the star turn of his time experiment, here at the zoo,' explains the tortoise.

'I think I need to speak to this Professor,' suggests the Doctor.

The tortoise tells you that you need to go to the Control Centre.

'I don't suppose you could show us where that is?' asks Martha, as sweetly as she can.

If the tortoise agrees to take you, go to 100. If the tortoise isn't sure, go to 73.

The Doctor is already leading the way back to the place the TARDIS landed.

You have to run to keep up with him.

'I don't understand?' you tell him breathlessly, 'Are we just going to leave?'

The Doctor stops, so suddenly that you run into him.

'Of course not,' he tells you, looking hurt at the very idea.

'So what are we doing?' you ask.

The Doctor starts walking again and you fall into step beside him.

'There is something seriously wrong here, something upsetting the time flow. I need to find the source and the best way of doing that might be to go back in time to a point before whatever it is started having that effect.'

The Time Crocodile is still with you. He asks to come with you in the TARDIS.

If you take him, go to 47. If you decide not to, go to 76.

16 You talk about it with Martha.

She's worried — if you can't find the Doctor you'll both be stuck here. For the moment it really doesn't look as if you have any choice but to trust the crocodile.

You are still unsure.

Martha asks you to think about what the Doctor would do. She knows you've only recently met him but she thinks you can tell what sort of a man he is. He likes to give people the benefit of the doubt.

If things had been reversed and she had been the one who had disappeared she is confident that he would do the same thing.

You decide that you have no choice but to see where the crocodile takes you for now.

Martha warns you to be ready for anything.

If you have picked up the stun blaster, go to 91. If you are unarmed, go to 23.

17 Inside the cage the Doctor looks at the crocodile with suspicion.

'No disrespect my friend, but maybe there's a reason you're locked in.'

The crocodile thrashes his tail angrily, splashing the water at the edge of his pool.

'I'm not what I appear to be,' he tells you, fuming.

'You're not a talking crocodile?' asks the Doctor.

'Obviously I'm a talking crocodile but I'm more than that. I told you, I'm the Time Crocodile. I can travel in time. At least I can usually.'

'But not inside this cage?' guesses the Doctor.

The crocodile nods his head. 'Too right. Stuffed with time buffers. The Professor doesn't want me going anywhere until...'

The crocodile never finishes as a blast of intense light goes off like a flashbulb.

When you open your eyes one of your companions has disappeared.

If it is the Doctor, go to 78. If it is Martha, go to 48.

18 Behind the glass of the nearest enclosure to the left is what appears to be a talking crocodile. You hurry to the Doctor's side and introduce yourselves to the creature.

'Tim,' the crocodile says back. 'Tim E. Crocodile but everyone calls me the Time Crocodile.'

'And why is that?' asks the Doctor.

'Because I can travel in time, of course,' snaps the crocodile haughtily.

'So what is this place and who's in charge?' demands the Doctor.

'No one's in charge. All the keepers have gone.' The crocodile sounds upset, almost on the verge of crying.

'Don't worry,' whispers the Doctor, 'they'll just be crocodile tears.'

'If you want to know anything else, either come in here or let me out. Take your pick.'

If you go into the cage to talk to the crocodile, go to 17. If you let him out, go to 110.

19 You put a plastic cup under the tap, press the button and what appears to be fresh clear water pours out.

You sniff it suspiciously but it does seem to be water. Your thirst gets the better of your caution and you take a sip.

On the wall you notice a framed academic certificate that belongs to someone called Thomas Morrow. The date on the certificate is 2345 — you're in the twenty-fourth century! You turn to tell the Doctor what you've discovered but are shocked to see that the Doctor has disappeared! You're on your own in the future!

A moment later he reappears, with Martha in tow. 'Thought we should all stick together,' he tells you and calls you to explore further before exiting through a door and leaving you alone again.

If you finish your drink before following, go to 4. If you hurry after them right away, go to 3.

'We must shut down this time experiment,' insists the ex-Time Crocodile.

The Doctor nods. 'But it has to be done in both time zones to cancel out the time spillage.'

You put your hand up. 'Sorry, too much techno-babble,' you complain. 'Can we have that in English?'

'The Professor's experiments have created a sort of bridge between here and the future,' he begins.

'And the bridge is constantly expanding,' adds the Time Crocodile.

'Which will cause more time distortion.'

'Unchecked it will get bigger and bigger until...'

'Boom?'

The Doctor nods at you. 'We need to get back to the TARDIS...'

'And "Back to the Future"?' you suggest.

'One of my favourite films,' the Doctor tells you.

If the TARDIS lands in the future in the same location as before, go to 57. If it lands in the Control Centre, go to 39.

Suddenly the room is plunged into darkness and someone pulls you to the floor.

'This way,' whispers the Doctor.

A couple of blasts of laser fire go off over your head and then you hear footsteps running away.

The Doctor switches the light back on.

'I couldn't see a thing,' you say.

'You should eat more carrots,' the Doctor tells you. 'We need to get back to the future.'

'I don't understand. I thought we needed to be at the start of the experiment to stop it?'

The Doctor shakes his head.

'I was wrong. Whatever it is at the heart of the time experiment isn't fixed in time itself. It's moving forward with the time bridge. I think it might be trying to get home...'

If the TARDIS lands back where it first landed, go to 57. If the TARDIS lands in the Control Centre, go to 39.

'I'm going to try and materialize the TARDIS around the Time Crocodile,' the Doctor tells you. 'As soon as you see even the faintest sign of him, tell me.'

You scan the vast orange and green chamber, looking for anything that might be the Time Crocodile. The massive uprights are like dinosaur bones reaching up to the distant dark ceiling. Suddenly you see a patch of air shimmering like a heat haze. 'Now Doctor!' you cry out and he slams down a sequence of levers. With a sudden jerk the time sensitive creature materializes.

'Where am I?' he asks, disorientated.

'This is a real time machine,' the Doctor tells him, 'Can't you feel it?'

The Time Crocodile begins to sway, as if dizzy. 'Oh yes,' he drawls, 'I can taste the time energy. It's filling me...'

Quickly the Doctor and the Professor explain about the wrecked time ship.

'But what can we do to stop it?' you ask.

The Doctor looks grim. 'The time ship leak has to be repaired and its engines topped up then it can return to wherever it came from.'

'And you need me to do that?' the Time Crocodile asks.

The Doctor nods. He adjusts some controls. 'Right,' he announces, 'I can't hold this position for very long.' He operates a switch and the twin police box doors open to reveal a strange blue glowing space beyond.

'Is this a one-way trip?' asks the Time Crocodile quietly.

'I don't know,' the Doctor confesses.

The crocodile walks to the doors then turns to address the Professor. 'Thanks Professor. For making me capable of this.'

He turns and enters the time ship. Instantly there is a massive explosion of multi-coloured light.

If the Time Crocodile disappears, go to 104.
If the Time Crocodile comes back, go to 71.

23 | The Time Crocodile leads you along a corridor.

'I don't understand,' you say, 'How did a zoo become a research centre?'

'It's a fake zoo,' the crocodile explains. 'All the animals are robots. It's a recreation of an old-fashioned zoo. There was a real fad for this sort of thing in the early 24th century, lots of different tourist attractions recreated classic old Earth favourites.'

'Like we have mock medieval pageants at places like Warwick Castle, I suppose,' you suggest.

'Trouble is,' continues the crocodile, 'fashion moved on. Suddenly the past was just too old-fashioned. Places like this were shutting down all over the place. The Professor picked this up cheap as a base for his time experiments. Here we are.'

You've reached a door marked Control. You push at the door.

If Martha is not with you, go to 34. If Martha is with you, go to 40.

The Doctor pulls out his sonic screwdriver and takes a reading.

He turns to the Professor. 'Can I get access to your experiment records from a terminal near here?'

The Professor takes out a pen from which he extracts a thin roll-up screen. At the press of a button the screen hardens, forming a pad-like computer.

'Neat,' you comment.

'It's a bit retro,' the Professor says sheepishly, 'Very last century!'

'Nevertheless, it does the job,' the Doctor tells him, as data rolls across the screen at a dizzying speed.

'What does it tell you?' asks Martha.

'Just as I thought,' the Doctor answers, 'There's a defunct time ship out there, or at least the remains of one, and it's leaking time particles. That is what has infected your animals. We have to find it and stop it.'

If this makes sense, go to 103. If it doesn't, go to 58.

'I need to have a good look at this Time Crocodile,' announces the Doctor.

The Professor nods. 'But who are you?'

'I'm the Doctor. I'm somewhat of an expert in matters of time travel. Born to it, you might say,' the Doctor tells him proudly.

'He can't seem to do it all the time,' explains the Professor.

'So there are certain times when he can travel in time? Regular times? And have you considered why?'

'No,' the Professor confesses.

'It must be connected to the movement of the space station.'

'But the station is in geostationary orbit. It doesn't move relative to the planet.'

'No, but the planet moves.'

A security monitor shows that the Time Crocodile's pen is completely empty — the Time Crocodile has disappeared.

If the Doctor decides to go back to the TARDIS, go to 92. If the Doctor decides to use his Sonic Screwdriver, go to 24.

'**I** can tell you're impressed!'

The speaker is a man in his forties, dressed in a white lab coat. 'I'm Professor Morrow,' he tells you.

In return the Doctor introduces you, Martha and himself.

'You're responsible for all this?' asks the Doctor with a hint of criticism in his voice. 'The enhanced animals, this zoo of experimental creatures?'

The Professor looks at him suspiciously.

'Don't tell me you're one of those tiresome animal rights types?'

The Doctor gives him a broad disarming smile.

'I'm just curious about what it is you do here,' he explains.

'I'm a geneticist. Lots of these old Earth creatures are all but extinct. I'm trying to save them.'

'Really. And you do that by tweaking their DNA and giving them human-like intelligence, do you?'

If you are in the lab, go to 60. If you are in or by a cage, go to 93.

| 'Come on then, say what you're thinking. "Oh look, a talking tortoise!" they always do.'

Determined not to admit your surprise you say nothing. The Doctor, of course, doesn't even blink. He just whips out his dark-rimmed glasses and bends to take a closer look.

'I don't like to waste time stating the obvious,' he tells the tortoise, 'But I am a bit of a stickler for accuracy and technically you're not really a talking tortoise are you? You're using some kind of low-level telepathy. Which is all very clever but not actually talking.'

The Doctor introduces your party and asks if the tortoise has a name.

'You can call me Five,' he says.

'Odd kind of name,' you comment.

'It's not a name. It's a designation.'

If this is the tortoise speaking, go to 94. If this is a new voice, go to 26.

'Look,' you cry out. 'It's a crocodile.' The Doctor and Martha join you. The crocodile is lying next to a muddy-looking pool of water.

'He doesn't look very happy does he?' you suggest.

'Who would be, stuck in here?' says the crocodile.

You and Martha are stunned.

'Did it just speak?' stutters Martha in amazement.

'Do you mind? I'm not an "it",' complains the crocodile.

The Doctor has crouched down to take a closer look at the creature.

'Ah, I see now. That device attached to your throat is actually providing the voice, right?'

The crocodile nods. 'Thanks to Professor Morrow's Vocaliser I can now express my thoughts.'

'Indeed you can,' agrees the Doctor getting to his feet, 'but the question is how did a crocodile get to be smart enough to have thoughts to express?'

If the crocodile answers your question, go to 94. If a new voice appears, go to 26.

29 | You step out of the TARDIS into darkness. After a moment your eyes begin to adjust to the gloom. There is some light but it's just a faint glow from the ceiling of the room.

There is a very strong smell in the room. It's an earthy, animal smell.

'Let's see if we can shed some light on this,' comments the Doctor as he and Martha emerge from the TARDIS behind you.

The Doctor flashes his sonic screwdriver and the lights start to brighten.

Now you can see that the floor is actually earthen and that one of the walls is entirely glass.

'We're in a cage!' you announce.

'Give the youth a prize!' drawls an unfamiliar voice sarcastically. 'What did you expect in a zoo? Hotel rooms?!'

If the speaker appears to be a tortoise, go to 27. If the speaker appears to be a crocodile, go to 61.

You and Martha creep unseen into the main lab. From a position of concealment you can see the Professor making his final checks.

'How do we stop him?' you whisper.

Before she can answer you the door opens and the Time Crocodile, holding the Doctor at gunpoint, enters. The Professor turns in surprise.

'What's going on? Why have you changed into your human form?'

'Comfort!' the Time Crocodile tells him.

Behind you the tortoise appears.

He too, like the Time Crocodile, has morphed into a humanoid and he's holding a weapon pointing directly at you.

'Sorry,' he mutters, 'We just can't let you interfere.'

'Don't do this,' the Doctor is almost pleading with the Professor. Ignoring him the Professor reaches for the controls. You spot a massive grey lever near you marked Power Override.

If you run and pull it, go to 65. If you dare not, go to 88.

The TARDIS has landed exactly where it did the first time, in the future. The Doctor leads you all out and sets off in the direction of the Control Centre.

'We have to get there before the Professor can begin the experiment,' he reminds you.

At the Control Centre you find that the Professor, looking calm and professional, is about to initialise his time experiment. The Doctor strides towards the door that leads to the lab. 'Stop right there,' someone orders. The speaker is a humanoid with a crocodile's head — the Time Crocodile!

'Listen to me,' the Doctor begins to explain to the Time Crocodile.

Seeing that the Time Crocodile is fully focused on the Doctor, Martha taps you on the shoulder and points to another door.

Martha reaches out to the handle and begins to open it.

If you escape without being noticed, go to 30. If you're spotted, go to 37.

The Time Crocodile has saved your life. You're lying on the floor and for a moment you can't see what's happening. You flip yourself over and see the Time Crocodile leaping towards the heart of the Professor's time experiment.

Above you the wall-mounted defence system is swivelling to take aim.

The laser fires but the Time Crocodile flickers as the laser beam passes through him, using his time travel powers to survive. He reaches the time experiment and smashes it with his tail. The room is filled with multi-coloured light, exploding like an indoor firework display.

For a moment you are blinded but slowly your sight returns. The lab is a scene of total destruction. The Time Crocodile has totally vanished.

'Are you all right?' a familiar voice asks you.

If it is Martha, go to 5. If it is the Doctor, go to 9.

Inside the TARDIS the Doctor hurries to the controls. 'This is going to be very fiddly,' he mutters, 'crossing back against one's own time line is a very dangerous activity. I'm going to be breaking half a dozen Laws of Time.'

The tortoise is looking around the TARDIS control room with a look of amazement.

'This is a time machine?'

'Oh it's more than that,' you tell him with a hint of pride. 'It can go anywhere in time and space.'

'When he can get it to do what he wants, that is!' Martha adds with a grin.

'I heard that,' says the Doctor from the console where he is hitting some controls with a wooden mallet. 'That should do it!' he adds. The TARDIS begins to land.

If it lands in the same spot as before, go to 31. If it lands in the Control Centre, go to 89.

34 The Control Centre is full of computers and screens. It looks a little like Mission Control for a NASA space flight but on a smaller scale. The Doctor has gone in first and is busy examining all the equipment.

'This must have originally been the zoo's security office,' he comments after a while.

'But where is the Professor?' you wonder.

'Over here,' calls the Time Crocodile, who has followed you into the room.

The Time Crocodile is by a locked door.

'What's behind there?' asks the Doctor.

'The Professor's private flat,' explains the Time Crocodile.

'Hello. Anyone at home?' calls the Doctor, banging on the door.

There is no answer.

'This is a time lock,' announces the Doctor. 'It's not going to open soon.'

If you decide to try and break down the door, go to 77. If you decide to go back to the TARDIS, go to 15.

You dash to the Doctor's coat and reach into the pocket. You find what he was asking for: a thick silver pen-like device — the sonic screwdriver!

You throw it to the Doctor, who catches it and aims it at a spot on the console.

Immediately there is a flash of sparks from the console and then everything returns to normal again.

The Doctor flashes you a grin.

'Thanks. I needed to tweak the time accelerator. We needed some extra oomph.'

'Why?' asks Martha.

The Doctor nods at the viewer screen. It shows a barren looking moon. The only sign of life is a habitat dome.

"Something to do with that dome. It's emitting some serious time distortion. Question is do we play cautious and land outside the dome or try and materialize inside?' he asks.

If you say outside, go to 41. If you answer in the dome, go to 50.

36 | The Time Crocodile begins to lead the way. You hold back and grab the Doctor's sleeve.

'Can we trust him?' you ask.

'I don't know,' confesses the Doctor, 'but I don't really see how we have a choice. Something is causing some serious disruptions to space and time around here and I need to find out what it is.'

'But what about Martha?'

'I haven't forgotten her,' the Doctor reassures you, 'but if I'm right she's perfectly safe, just slightly dislocated in time.'

'So has she travelled in time?'

'In a way. I think she's been jarred a split-second into the future. She's constantly just that moment ahead of us. If I can find the source of the disruption I should be able to put it right...'

If you want to know more about this zoo, go to 109. If you're happy to wait and see what happens, go to 23.

'Don't think about going in to warn him,' says the tortoise.

You turn and see that he too, like the Time Crocodile, has morphed into a new shape. Now humanoid, he's holding a weapon pointing directly at you.

'I don't understand,' you say.

The Doctor explains, 'They're alien shape-shifters — the Lalunis I suspect. Desperate for time technology. Everything they've told us up to now has been a lie.'

He turns to face the aliens. 'You have to let me stop this before its too late,' he tells them earnestly.

Inside the inner room the Professor is about to turn his machine on.

'Last chance,' the Doctor announces, 'we have to shut off the power to that room with the override on the wall,' he adds, pointing at a massive grey lever near you.

If you run and pull it, go to 65. If you dare not, go to 88.

38 | The Professor falls to the ground.

'I'm sorry but I can't allow you to stop this experiment,' explains a gruff voice. It is a powerful-looking humanoid with a crocodile's head — the so-called Time Crocodile.

'I tried the traditional croc look for a bit,' he informs you, 'but I got bored with the crawling!'

'But there was no need to kill the Professor.'

'It's just a stun setting,' insists the Time Crocodile. 'I'm not a killer.'

'You will be if you stop me shutting this abomination down,' the Doctor replies.

The crocodile ignores him and presses a control. Instantly a golden portal of light appears and the Time Crocodile steps through and disappears.

The Doctor is impressed. 'That's a time tunnel,' he tells you. 'He's moving backwards or forwards in time. We have to follow him!'

If you follow him through the portal, go to 89.
If you decide to take the TARDIS, go to 33.

The TARDIS has materialized inside the Professor's lab in the zoo's Control Centre. As you exit through the police box doors a ceiling-mounted defence laser hums into life. It fires but misses as the Doctor pulls you down to a place of concealment, clear of the line of fire.

He points at a particular console at the far side of the room.

'When I distract the auto defence AI, run and disable that unit.'

'How?' you ask.

'Improvise,' suggests the Doctor. 'I always do!'

With that the Doctor jumps to his feet and begins running in a manic zigzagging fashion. 'Go!' he shouts at you.

You jump up and begin to run but the laser turns to target you.

Someone shoves you in the back and you go flying.

If the Time Croc is your ally, go to 32. If the Time Croc is a villain, go to 108.

40 The door opens and you enter a room full of computers and other scientific equipment.

'I think this was originally the security centre, but Professor Morrow made it his centre of operations,' explains the Time Crocodile.

'Something's going on,' you suggest, looking at the screens, which show numbers scrolling down at impossible speeds.

Martha joins you. 'Could be running some sort of programme, or it might just be a virus checker?'

'Professor Morrow would know.'

'But we don't know where to find him,' replies Martha annoyed.

Suddenly the air shimmers as if in a heat haze and in a shower of flickering colours the crocodile disappears.

You and Martha exchange a look and shrug.

'I guess we're on our own,' you comment, 'Where now?'

'Through there?' suggests Martha, waving towards an inner door.

If you want to go first, go to 87. If you want Martha to go first, go to 99.

41 'It's no good,' the Doctor tells you, after wrestling with the controls for a few minutes, 'the time distortion is preventing me from landing on the surface... I'll have to try and break through and land inside the dome.'

A few moments later the TARDIS begins to materialize and within minutes you find yourself following the Doctor and Martha out of the police box into what appears to be a zoo.

You spread out slightly to explore. You spot some kind of futuristic weapon on the ground and are unsure whether or not to pick it up.

You think about asking the Doctor and see that he is disappearing around a corner. When you get to the corner you see that he has gone through one of two doorways.

If you find the Doctor through the left door, go to 3. If you find him through the right door, go to 4.

'That must be your other companion, Doctor.'

You look to see who or what is speaking. The Doctor is standing near to one of the animal enclosures. Behind him is a large crocodile.

'Look out!' you cry, pointing at the crocodile.

'Don't you know it's rude to point?' asks the crocodile.

'Meet Tim,' says the Doctor, grinning, 'He's a Time Crocodile.'

'The Time Crocodile,' the creature corrects the Doctor, 'The One and Only.'

'And what is the Time Crocodile?' you ask, hesitantly.

The Doctor looks down at the crocodile, who shuffles in an embarrassed manner. 'A time-sensitive shape-shifter, am I right?'

'Perhaps.'

'And are you the reason for the time distortion my instruments picked up?' asks the Doctor?

'No. They're the reason I'm here.'

If you trust the Time Crocodile go to 110.
If you are suspicious of him go to 17.

43 | Moments later the doors open again and Martha comes back into the TARDIS.

'Nothing's happened,' you tell her, pointing at the monitor.

'Don't worry about it,' she tells you, 'The Doctor thinks it's probably safer if you stick with us. Come on...'

'But what about the time distort readings? I thought the Doctor needed someone to monitor them?'

Martha explains that the Doctor has changed his mind. 'He does that, you know. You have to stay on your toes to keep up.'

As you cross the control room you ask her what is out there. 'Any aliens?' you ask, enthusiastically.

'Come and see for yourself,' she says, adding, 'It's a sort of zoo.'

'A zoo?' you reply, surprised. 'With animals?'

She grins and nods her head as she opens the door.

If you step out ahead of her, go to 42. If you let Martha go first, go to 95.

44 The Doctor and Martha look at each other. You wonder if you've overstepped the mark.

'Look if I'm going to be in the way...' you begin. 'I don't want to be a gooseberry. If you two prefer to travel alone...' you continue.

'Well, no, it's not that,' the Doctor tries to explain.

'It's just that it can be dangerous,' says Martha.

'You're okay though, aren't you?' you ask Martha.

'Just about,' she admits.

You turn to the Doctor, realising that it's his space/time machine and his decision to make.

'I only take the best,' he explains gravely, but there's a twinkle in his eyes that he can't hide. 'And it's just one trip,' he continues, 'you've got school tomorrow, haven't you?'

If you admit that you need to be back for school, go to 69. If you lie and tell the Doctor you don't need to go back, go to 82.

You feel a bit dizzy and everything becomes a bit of a blur. You close your eyes and shake your head. When you open your eyes everything is back to normal. At first you're not sure that you've travelled at all but then you realise that the zoo lights are on, simulating full daylight.

The only signs of life are squat white robots with multiple arms that whizz around silently. When they first appear you are concerned but the Time Crocodile assures you that these are just simple maintenance robots.

'They're the zoo keepers,' he explains.

'No sign of the TARDIS,' you comment, as you climb off his back.

'Maybe he landed somewhere else,' he suggests.

Now you're back in the past with the Time Crocodile you're not sure what your next move should be.

If you decide to ask the Time Crocodile, go to 72. If you decide to go to the Control Centre, go to 106.

46 | The TARDIS engines die down and the Doctor checks the scanner.

'Excellent, ' he announces. 'We've landed in exactly the same place in the zoo as before, only about forty eight hours earlier.'

'Is that far enough back?' you ask.

The Doctor nods. 'I'm getting a reading of a much lower level of time particles present which suggests that the full time corridor experiment hasn't been started yet. Shall we get going?'

'How are we going to stop the Professor's experiment?' you ask.

'Oh, I don't know,' the Doctor tells you, 'I don't like to have too much of a plan. I prefer to see where things take me.'

He heads for the double doors.

'We need to get to the Control Centre as quickly as possible,' he reminds you. 'Do you remember the way?'

If you do remember the way, go to 10. If you're not sure, go to 12.

You get inside the TARDIS and the Doctor goes straight to the console and begins adjusting the flight settings. It feels odd to be in here about to take off without Martha.

'Impressive,' drawls the Time Crocodile looking around.

'Thank you,' replies the Doctor.

'Of course, it's all a bit over the top.'

'Over the top?!' repeats the Doctor, affronted.

'All this... technology. I can travel through time without any of this.'

The Doctor gives him a cool look. 'Really?'

'Yes.'

'Then why don't you? We'll meet you there.'

The Time Crocodile looks away.

'Can't,' he mutters. 'Time distortion,' he adds.

'No time distortion is going to stop my TARDIS,' states the

Doctor, as the TARDIS engines start up. Immediately the space/time craft begins to shake.

'Quickly, pull that lever,' the Doctor asks you pointing.

If you reach the lever, go to 46. If you can't move the lever, go to 6.

'Doctor!'

You shout out but it's too late. Martha has gone — vanished in a blast of intense light.

'What happened to her? Is she...?' You let your voice trail off, horrified at the thought.

The Doctor looks grim-faced, but not too upset. You find this strangely reassuring.

'Don't panic. Martha is fine.'

'But where is she?' you demand, anxiously.

'Still here, but displaced in time by a micro-second or two,' offers the crocodile.

The Doctor rounds on him, raising a quizzical eyebrow.

'You know something of temporal mechanics?' he asks, surprised.

'Of course I do. I'm the Time Crocodile. Time travel is what I was built for.'

'Can you help us get her back?' asks the Doctor.

'Of course. Let me take you to the Professor.'

If you think you should do this, go to 23. If you think you should be more cautious, go to 36.

49 You bend down and tap politely on the shell of the tortoise.

'Excuse me,' you ask, 'but I wonder if you can help us?'

The tortoise pops his head out.

'How do I know I can trust you?' he asks, suspiciously.

'Please,' you say, 'we just want to know what's going on.'

'You need to talk to Professor Morrow then,' answers the tortoise, tartly. 'Or the Time Crocodile.'

'The what?' you ask.

'The Time Croc is the Professor's pet — the star turn of his time experiment,' explains the tortoise.

'I think I need to speak to this Professor,' suggests the Doctor.

The tortoise tells you that you need to go to the Control Centre.

'I don't suppose you could show us where that is?' asks Martha, as sweetly as she can.

If the tortoise agrees to take you, go to 100. If the tortoise isn't sure, go to 73.

The TARDIS has materialized somewhere inside the mysterious dome.

You have followed the Doctor and Martha out into what appears to be an entrance hall to something. There are ticket booths and turnstiles.

'It's a zoo! Look,' exclaims Martha, who has been looking at a wall map.

'Let's go and look around,' suggests the Doctor, waving his sonic screwdriver at the nearest turnstile and walking through.

The three of you separate slightly to explore. You find what appears to be a futuristic weapon on the ground and are unsure whether or not to pick it up.

You think about asking the Doctor and see that he is disappearing around a corner. You hurry to catch him up but he has disappeared through one of two doorways.

If you find the Doctor through the left door, go to 3. If you find him through the right door, go to 4.

51 'Is it dangerous?' you ask.

The Doctor shrugs. 'Won't know until we look, will we?' He winks at you and then turns to Martha.

'Maybe it's best if you keep an eye on the time distort reader.'

Martha looks a bit annoyed.

'It's very important,' the Doctor tells her. The Doctor indicates one of the screens on the console. 'This displays the level of time distortion. Usually I'd expect a background level of around 0.5, 0.6 but as you can see it's up around the 175 mark.'

'And that's bad?' Martha asks.

'Possibly, but whatever it is, I need to know,' answers the Doctor. 'If it goes over 200 hit reset, enter 451 and wait.'

He takes you to the door and opens it for you. 'Would you like to go first?'

If you go out first, go to 67. If you prefer to follow the Doctor, go to 81.

You dash to the Doctor's coat and reach into the pocket. You find what the Doctor was looking for — an ordinary-looking key on a piece of string.

You throw it to the Doctor, who catches it and puts into a slot on the console.

Immediately there is a sudden burst of extra engine sounds and then the space/time craft seems to come under control again.

The Doctor flashes you a grin.

'Thanks. The key doubles as a battery, we needed some extra oomph.'

'Why?' asks Martha.

The Doctor nods at the viewer screen. It shows a barren-looking moon. The only sign of life is a habitat dome.

'Something to do with that dome. Question is: do we play cautious and land outside the dome or try and materialize inside?' he asks.

If you say 'outside', go to 55. If you answer 'in the dome', go to 97.

'I'm not surprised,' Martha tells you, 'I'd think twice about it too.'

The Doctor raises an eyebrow. 'Are you suggesting my ship isn't safe?' he asks in a hurt tone.

'Of course not,' replies Martha and winks at you behind the Doctor's back.

After a few minutes you arrive. The TV screen flickers into life and shows an image of the park where you first spotted the TARDIS.

'There you are, home again!' Martha tells you with a smile.

'And just a few minutes after you left,' adds the Doctor, 'to avoid any awkward questions.' He walks you to the doors.

'Can I come again some time?' you ask him as you leave.

'Who knows?' smiles the Doctor. 'Time will tell... It usually does.'

The TARDIS engines begin to roar and, as you turn back to watch, the TARDIS elegantly fades from sight.

Your adventure in time and space is over.

You try banging on the glass of the enclosure and the tortoise looks up briefly and then carries on chewing his lettuce lunch.

'Hey? Can you hear me?' you shout through the glass, but there is no reply. You run to the next enclosure where a pair of giraffes are grazing.

You try talking to them instead. The giraffes just look down their long necks at you, haughtily, and then ignore you.

'It's no good — they're dumb,' Tim, the Time Crocodile, tells you.

You frown. 'But I thought the animals in this zoo could talk?'

'Why would you think that?'

'Because you can talk, I suppose,'

The Time Crocodile shakes his head.

'Dodgy logic, young tellurian, dodgy logic... Now come on...'

If the Doctor is with you at the moment you should go directly to the Control Centre at 10. But if the Doctor is not with you, go to 72.

55 You and Martha watch as the Doctor rushes around the central console flicking switches and pulling levers. 'Is there anything we can do?' you ask. 'Just stand back and admire my driving skills,' the Doctor tells you with a laugh. Just then the TARDIS rocks violently.

'Oh behave,' complains the Doctor, 'I think she's cross with me for showing off,' he explains, patting the console apologetically.

He checks some readings and sighs heavily. 'It's no good,' he announces, 'I can't materialize because of the time distortion. But I think I can land inside unnoticed.'

A few moments later the TARDIS has materialized and you are ready to go out and explore.

The Doctor asks one of you to stay in the TARDIS to check the time distort reader.

You and Martha exchange a look.

If you suggest Martha should stay, go to 51. If you volunteer to stay, go to 68.

'I knew there was something odd about him,' you mutter.

Before your eyes an amazing transformation is taking place. Somehow the Time Crocodile's rear legs are growing, extending, lengthening. 'It's a shape-shifter...' explains the Doctor.

'Do you mind not talking about me as if I'm not here?' demands the alien creature, now humanoid in shape. Despite the change it still has a reptilian scaly skin and the head of a crocodile.

'A Khellian?' The Doctor asks.

The creature laughs. 'Certainly not. Just a more convenient body. I cannot return to my natural form without the aid of my ship but I can... rearrange this form.'

'So who are you?'

'I'm Trahlen of the Lalunis and I am here to stop this madness. And thanks to your intervention I now know exactly what I need to do.'

If the Professor is dead, go to 21. If the Professor is alive, go to 20.

57 | The TARDIS has returned to the same place in the zoo that it first landed. You hurry out, heading for the Professor's lab. As you move through the now familiar layout of the zoo alarms begin to sound.

'What's happening?' you ask the Doctor.

'Oh the usual, security systems, alarms, that sort of thing.'

Even as he speaks, the lights go out and are replaced by flashing red emergency lighting. Sliding security barriers begin to close off various routes. The Doctor uses his sonic screwdriver to stop and reverse the barriers.

'When we get to the Control Centre,' the Doctor tells you, 'Start turning off everything you can.'

You look up as a wall-mounted camera swings around to point at you. A gun barrel emerges from the casing and begins to fire in your direction.

If the Time Crocodile saves you, go to 32. If the Doctor saves you, go to 108.

'There's a rip in space time,' explains the Doctor. 'Well, more of a hole, a puncture...'

'Like a pin prick in a paddling pool?'

'Exactly. And it's beginning to tear. More and more time particles are pouring out.'

'But how did the time particles infect the animals?' you ask.

'I don't know,' the Doctor confesses, 'But at a guess something in the genetic enhancement work that the Professor was doing created a susceptibility to this kind of infection. Certain biological processes do have sympathetic resonance to time particles.'

'Getting a bit techno-babble now,' you warn him.

'Sorry,' says the Doctor, 'suffice to say it's a bit like a chemical plant pouring waste into a river. You need to stop it before you kill all the fish.'

If you think a time ship is causing the problem, go to 22. If you think a natural time/space flux is the problem, go to 103.

59 'Where is this Time Crocodile?' announces the Doctor, 'I need to see him for myself.'

'He'll be in his cage,' the Professor tells you. 'But why should I let you near him? Who are you?'

'He's a Time Lord. He knows all about time travel,' you tell him.

'A Time Lord? What's that?' he asks.

'My people know more about time travel than the rest of the universe put together. The Time Lords used to enforce the Laws of Time,' the Doctor tells him. 'Unfortunately I'm the only one left now to clear up little problems like this.'

The Professor starts taking you all back through the zoo to the crocodile pen but when you get there, it is empty. The crocodile has disappeared.

> **If the Doctor decides to go back to the TARDIS, go to 92. If the Doctor pulls out his sonic screwdriver, go to 24.**

60 The Professor looks unhappy.

'You may have your doubts about my work, but believe me I do have the animals' best interests at heart.'

'Do you?'

'There is a problem though...'

The Doctor raises an eyebrow but says nothing as the Professor leads you away from the cages and back into the main lab.

'Something has compromised my security,' he explains, closing the door behind you.

'An intruder?' asks Martha.

'No, but something's influenced the outcome of my recent experiments. It's created a crocodile that can move through time at will.'

'Are you serious?'

The Professor nods. 'It seems normal to look at but it travels in time. It's unsettling.'

'It's more than that,' the Doctor tells him, 'it's downright dangerous. Casual time travel like that could damage the space-time continuum.'

If you've met the Time Crocodile, go to 25. If you've not met the Time Crocodile, go to 59.

You can't quite believe that a talking crocodile has addressed you but the Doctor doesn't seem to be at all surprised. He whips out his dark-rimmed glasses and bends to take a closer look at the creature.

'How can a crocodile speak?' you ask.

'Technically he can't,' the Doctor answers.

'Are you all imagining me then?'

'Strictly speaking,' the Doctor tells the crocodile, 'you're not really talking; you're just using some kind of low-level telepathy.'

The Doctor introduces you, Martha and himself and wonders if the crocodile has a name.

'Officially I am known as Four,' he says.

'Odd kind of name,' you comment.

'It's not my name. It's my number. I'm experiment Four.'

The Doctor nods as if this confirms something he was thinking.

'Alternatively known as the Time Crocodile!'

If this is the crocodile speaking, go to 94. If this is a new voice, go to 26.

'If the time disturbance came from the space station will it make it difficult for you to land?' you ask.

'Good question,' the Doctor tells you. 'Let's see...' He tweaks some controls and then looks you in the eye.

'Whatever caused those problems it seems to have stopped for the moment. So if we're quick...' he trails off and in a blistering burst of speed operates half a dozen controls in a blink of an eye, 'we should be able to slip in without any trouble.'

With that the Doctor slams down a final lever, the engine noises fade and he announces that you've arrived.

He quickly checks that it is safe to explore and suggests that you might like to lead the way.

If you decide to lead the way out of the TARDIS, go to 29. If you prefer to follow the Doctor and Martha, go to 95.

Suddenly the TARDIS stops tossing and turning.

'Sorry,' says Martha, hurriedly rolling off you and blushing. 'Are you all right?'

You dust yourself down. 'I think I'm okay,' you tell her. The Doctor looks over at the pair of you. 'If you've quite finished playing sardines you might want to come and have a look at this,' he suggests.

On the screen you can see a large space station, hanging in geostationary orbit above an Earth-like world.

'That's the centre of the time distortion that the TARDIS detected,' announces the Doctor.

'Should we take a closer look?' asks Martha.

The Doctor reaches for a lever and then stops and looks directly at you.

'What do you think?' he asks you.

> If you think you should try and materialize directly inside the space station, go to 84.
> If you think you should get closer and take more readings, go to 62.

64 'Look,' you say, pointing at the flashing light blinking away on the console, 'is that meant to happen?'

The Doctor glances and shrugs nonchalantly. 'Oh, I wouldn't worry about that. I'm always getting flashing lights, never know what half of them mean!'

Just then a deep throbbing siren starts to sound, rising and falling in rhythm with the flashing warning light.

'Now I do know,' the Doctor continues, suddenly hurrying back to the controls of his time ship, 'and it's not good.'

You and Martha join the Doctor.

He yanks a control and sets the TARDIS in motion. 'If we're not careful we're going to be sucked into a time squall.'

'Is that dangerous?' Martha asks.

'About as mad as surfing in a hurricane,' the Doctor tells you.

You are hurled to the floor.

If you land under Martha, go to 63. If you land on Martha, go to 85.

You pull down the switch and turn off the power. 'No!' scream the aliens as the Doctor activates a setting on his sonic screwdriver. The Time Crocodile and the tortoise clutch their heads and collapse unconscious in a heap on the floor.

'I'm sorry,' the Doctor tells the Professor, 'but I really do have to stop this right here.'

The Professor watches as the Doctor unlocks a glass case at the centre of the machine from which a glowing ball of light emerges. The ball floats out of the Doctor's hands and morphs into a beautiful humanoid figure. It looks like a glowing statue. The creature introduces himself as a Time Agent from the far future.

'Thank you for rescuing me,' he tells the Doctor.

'I had no idea it was intelligent,' the Professor mutters desperately.

The Doctor nods at the Time Agent. 'I think he's telling the truth.'

'Nevertheless, he has gained knowledge of time mechanics that he cannot be allowed to keep. I shall have to remove part of his memory.' The glowing creature puts his hand on the Professor's forehead and the Professor collapses into the Doctor's arms.

'When he wakes, he'll remember nothing.'

The Time Agent turns to look at you and Martha. 'I'll handle them,' promises the Doctor quickly. The alien regards the Doctor for a long moment and then nods. Then the Time Agent disappears in another flash of multi-coloured light taking the tortoise and crocodile with him.

'Right then,' announces the Doctor, 'Time for us to make a move. We don't want to be here when the Professor wakes up, do we...?' You follow him back to the TARDIS.

Back inside the ship the Doctor offers you the chance to launch your final TARDIS journey.

If you accept, go to 70. If you decline, go to 53.

| Martha and the tortoise hurry towards you.

'Professor Morrow's shooting at us,' says the tortoise. 'He's totally lost his mind.'

'That's not all he's going to lose,' the Doctor replies. ' If we can't shut down his amateur attempt at time travel this whole place is going to be trapped in a time loop.'

'What can we do?' you ask.

'We need to get back to the TARDIS. I have to get to the exact point in time the experiment started.' The Doctor grins wildly. 'Time is of the essence!'

'I'm not built for speed,' the tortoise mutters. 'Go on without me.'

'No, you might be useful,' the Doctor tells him.

You spot an electric truck used to take supplies round the zoo. 'Could this help?'

If you use the truck to get back to the TARDIS, go to 33. If Professor Morrow finds you, go to 90.

67 You step through the doorway into darkness. You can just make out another open door nearby. You step through the second door and your eyes begin to adjust to the gloom. There is some light in here and you can see that one wall of the room seems to be made entirely of glass.

There is a very strong smell in the room. It's an earthy, animal smell. You look down and see that the floor is actually earthen. This is some kind of cage.

Is that the sound of something breathing or merely an air-conditioning fan?

Suddenly the lights come on and the Doctor is there, Martha with him.

'I thought we should explore this place together,' he explains and heads off again.

Martha gives you a grin. 'Come on then,' she urges you.

If Martha lets you go first, go to 4. If you let Martha go first, go to 3.

The Doctor makes some final checks and then he and Martha head for the police doors that lead to... wherever it is you've landed.

'Just keep checking that screen,' the Doctor reminds you. 'If the time distort reading goes over 200, hit reset, input code 451 and wait for me to come back. You should be safe in here.'

'Should be?' you repeat, worried.

'He means "will be", of course. Don't worry,' Martha smiles at you and then follows the Doctor out of the doors.

As the doors close behind them you realise how exciting this is. You're alone in a fantastic space/time vehicle. You see a door leading off into other rooms and wonder about exploring but remember that you have a job to do.

You look at the monitor screen.

If the reading is below 200, go to 43. If the reading is above 200, go to 80.

The Doctor smiles and begins to operate the controls.

'Just one quick trip then. Right then let's see... Where shall we go? Somewhere fun... the future or the past?'

You're bursting with ideas and suggestions but it's clear that the Doctor is talking to himself.

Suddenly everything goes crazy, the TARDIS rocks madly like a ship in a storm and you are thrown from side to side. Martha grabs hold of you and stops you from getting hurt.

Alarm bells and other sirens are sounding, making an awful noise. The Doctor is shouting something from the console and gesturing towards his brown coat, which is lying over a railing.

He wants you to get something from the coat pocket but it's hard to hear his exact words.

If you think he wants you to fetch the spare TARDIS key, go to 52. If you think he wants you to find the sonic screwdriver, go to 35.

70 | The TARDIS begins to shake and you stumble to the floor.

'Don't panic,' the Doctor assures you, 'it's perfectly normal!' As he speaks, something sparks on one of the consoles and he grabs a small fire extinguisher and shoots a blast of foam onto the smoking control.

Martha helps you to your feet.

'It isn't always like this,' Martha assures you, 'Just nine times out of ten!'

The engine noise gets even louder and a peculiar trumpeting begins to echo through the chamber. Suddenly there's a loud bang and then everything is silent.

The Doctor flicks a switch to activate a scanner. The TV screen flickers into life and shows an image of the park where you first spotted the TARDIS.

'There you are, home again!' Martha tells you with a smile.

'And just a few minutes after you left,' adds the Doctor.

'That's impossible,' you mutter, causing Martha and the Doctor to laugh again.

'Nothing's impossible when you have a TARDIS,' the Doctor says proudly. 'Well, almost nothing.'

'Your parking could do with a little work,' comments Martha.

'Okay, I'll give you that,' admits the Doctor.

'And your steering,' adds Martha with a grin.

The Doctor says nothing but raises an annoyed eyebrow. 'And don't get me started on the food machine,' continues Martha.

The Doctor ushers you to the door.

'I think it's time you were on your way,' he tells you. 'This could go on for a long time.'

You walk out of the doors and find yourself back in the park. The TARDIS engines begin to roar and, as you turn back to watch, the TARDIS elegantly fades from sight until there is nothing left except the flashing light on its roof. And then that, too, disappears.

Your adventure in time and space is over.

The Time Crocodile is now glowing with the same blue light as the time ship. Before your amazed eyes he begins to change shape. When the transformation is complete he looks like a human/crocodile hybrid.

'Thank you Doctor,' he says.

'My pleasure,' the Doctor tells him. 'May I know who it is that I've helped today?'

'I am Ophursis, a traveller from a distant time. When my ship was damaged I was scattered into fragments but I was able to survive in the DNA samples the Professor was developing and thus kept myself alive until I could find a way back to my ship and home. Thank you. Goodbye.'

The time ship vanishes and the Doctor returns the Professor to the zoo. After saying your goodbyes, the Doctor offers you the chance to launch your final TARDIS journey.

If you accept, go to 70. If you decline, go to 53.

The Time Crocodile suggests that you need to find the Professor and that the obvious place to start looking for him is in the Control Centre. You agree and set off purposefully through the zoo, confident of the geography now.

'The Professor is trying to generate a time bridge,' explains the Time Crocodile as you walk, 'He's managed to get hold of something that has travelled through time.'

'I don't understand,' you confess.

The Time Crocodile sighs.

'I'll keep this simple for you. Anything that travels through time picks up time particles — little bits of the Time Vortex. If you're clever enough — or mad enough — you can use them to create a crude time machine...'

'And is it dangerous?' you ask.

'Extremely! Which is why we need to reach the Control Centre!'

If the Doctor is with you, go to 10. If the Doctor is not with you, go to 106.

73 The tortoise begins to disappear into his home again.

'Please don't be afraid,' you cry out, 'we don't want to hurt you.'

The tortoise's head stops, halfway back inside his shell.

The Doctor crouches down to look the tortoise in the eyes.

'There's something wrong here, isn't there?' he states. 'I can sense it. If you help us, maybe we can put it right.'

Slowly, cautiously, the tortoise cranes his head to look at all three of you, one at a time.

'There have been some strange things going on. Bad things...' he whispers, looking around in a paranoid fashion.

'Then let us help,' insists the Doctor.

There is a long pause while the tortoise thinks it over. Finally he nods his head.

'I'll take you to the Control Centre,' he tells you solemnly.

Take a coin and toss it. If it's heads, go to 100. If it's tails, go to 8.

Another security door has just slammed shut in front of you but the Doctor points his sonic screwdriver at the controls and it begins to rise again.

You and the Doctor roll low on the floor under the opening door. As soon as you are through, the Doctor turns and makes the door seal again.

'Who was that?' you ask. 'Professor Morrow?'

The Doctor nods. 'Didn't seem too happy to see us, did he?'

You mention that he almost seemed scared. 'Why would anyone be frightened of us?'

The Doctor shrugs. 'Good question. Perhaps he's just a naturally suspicious person.'

You shake your head. 'He seemed totally paranoid.'

The Doctor has reached another security door and uses the sonic screwdriver to open it. The door starts to rise.

If it rises to reveal Martha and the tortoise, go to 66. If it rises to reveal Professor Morrow, go to 2.

As you step outside of the TARDIS the Time Crocodile is waiting for you.

'Thought better of it, did you?'

You shrug and then turn as the TARDIS engines roar into life and the Doctor's space/time craft fades from view.

Suddenly you feel very alone. Your only link with your own world, with your own time, has just disappeared leaving you in this unearthly alien zoo with only a talking crocodile for company.

'No, come back,' you cry out but it is too late. The TARDIS has vanished and the echoes of its engines are fading to silence.

'You want to try and follow?' offers the Time Crocodile.

'I thought you couldn't do that,' you say.

The crocodile looks away. 'Maybe I wasn't being entirely truthful,' he confesses. 'If you want me to try I can.'

If you accept his offer, go to 7. If you refuse, go to 86.

76 The Doctor enters the TARDIS and closes the doors on the Time Crocodile.

'He took that well,' you comment.

The Doctor nods, 'Too well.'

He runs up to the console and begins setting the controls for take-off.

'What about Martha?' you ask.

'If we get this right, we'll come back for her.'

'If?' You try to look the Doctor in the eye.

'I can't tell you that this isn't dangerous,' the Doctor tells you gravely. 'In strict terms it's against all the rules of time travel...'

'But you can do it?'

'I can try. Whatever's going on here has disrupted normal space/time so much that anything's possible.'

The Doctor looks at you and noticing your expression he asks you if you'd prefer not to go with him.

If you decide to go with the Doctor, go to 46.
If you decide to stay in the zoo, go to 75.

'Couldn't we try and break the door down?' you ask.

The Doctor nods and looks around for something to use as a battering ram.

'I think I know how to do this,' says the Doctor. As you watch the Doctor raises one leg and then kicks out at the door.

'Ow!' cries the Doctor and starts rubbing his ankle. 'That was a really bad idea.'

'I could have told you that,' adds the crocodile, with what sounds like a hint of laughter in his voice, 'that door's tougher than it looks.'

The Doctor looks a bit miffed. 'Yeah, I noticed,' he mutters. 'Right then, there's only one way to deal with this. We need to go back to the TARDIS.'

'Can I come?' asks the Time Crocodile.

'What do you think?' the Doctor asks you.

If you say yes, go to 47. If you say no, go to 76.

'**W**hat just happened?' you ask.

'I don't know,' confesses Martha, 'There was this bright light and then when I could see again the Doctor was gone.'

'Time quake,' says the Time Crocodile. 'A burst of Time Energy.'

'So where is the Doctor now?' Martha demands.

'More a question of when to be honest,' the crocodile replies.

'How did this happen?' you wonder.

The crocodile sighs. 'It's the Professor. He's trying to find a way to get organic material to travel in time. That's why I'm here.'

'To help him?'

'To stop him. I'm a kind of Time Cop.'

'A Time Agent?' asks Martha.

'Yeah, if you like. But it's time for me to blow my cover and act. If I can get to the Control Centre I should be able to track down your friend.'

If you trust him, go to 23. If you don't trust him, go to 16.

'Hey!' It's not immediately clear who – or what – is speaking. 'I'm down here,' the stranger says. You look down and see that it is a large tortoise talking to you.

'I'm sorry,' you find yourself saying, 'I didn't see you down there. What can I do for you?' you ask politely.

'Don't trust anyone here,' he almost whispers.

'What are you talking about?' demands Martha, a little impatiently.

The tortoise looks around with a paranoid air.

'Walls have ears,' he whispers and disappears into his shell.

'Well that didn't go too well, did it?' Martha comments.

The Doctor, who has been examining an information board nearby, joins you both.

'Did I hear our shell-bound friend here speaking?' he asks.

'He didn't say very much,' you explain.

'Really?' says the Doctor. 'That's a shame.'

If the Doctor tries to talk to the tortoise go to 14. If you address the tortoise go to 49.

You are walking towards the TARDIS doors when they burst open and the Doctor appears.

'Did the reading surge just now?' he asks, 'About thirty seconds ago?'

You nod.

'I thought so,' mutters the Doctor. He consults some readings on the console and then jumps up again. 'Right then,' he announces, 'change of plan. I think it's probably safer if we stick together. Come on...'

He heads off towards the doors again.

'But what about the time distort readings?' you ask.

'We'll do that on the hoof,' explains the Doctor.

As you cross the control room you ask him what to expect 'Any aliens?' you ask, enthusiastically.

'Come and see for yourself,' he replies with a grin, adding 'It's a sort of zoo.'

'A zoo?' you reply, surprised.

He takes you to the doors. If you exit first, go to 4. If the Doctor leads the way, go to 3.

You follow the Doctor and find yourselves in what looks like an office. There are desks, chairs, even a potted plant.

'This looks like the school office,' you state, unable to keep the disappointment out of your voice.

'Not a school — a zoo,' says the Doctor, pointing at a sign.

He bounces up and down. 'Gravity about 0.9 of Earth's. Now that's just not possible on a moon this size. Must be an artificial gravity generator somewhere. Which means someone has a really hefty power bill.'

He wanders off towards a door, which he opens and goes through. Meanwhile your attention is caught by something familiar in the opposite corner of the room — a water cooler! You realise that you are very thirsty.

If you decide to try and have a drink, go to 19. If you decide to follow the Doctor through the door, go to 67.

The Doctor raises a suspicious eyebrow. You confess that you do need to get back.

'But I hope there's time for a quick trip somewhere first?' you add, cheekily.

Before anything else can be said the TARDIS begins to shake uncontrollably. The ship is being buffeted by something very strong; it's like being in a tornado.

'I need to make an emergency dematerialisation,' announces the Doctor, 'Brace yourselves.'

Suddenly it feels as if the TARDIS has flipped in a 360-degree circle and then with a bang everything becomes still.

'I feel like I've been in a blender,' mutters Martha.

The Doctor is checking out his instruments.

'I need one of you to stay in here while we explore,' the Doctor tells you both, but he's looking directly at you.

If you volunteer to stay, go to 68. If you're not sure whether to go with the Doctor, go to 51.

You and Martha watch as the Doctor rushes around the central console flicking switches and pulling levers. 'Is there anything we can do?' you ask.

'Just stand back and admire my driving skills,' the Doctor tells you with a laugh. Just then the TARDIS rocks violently.

'Oh, behave,' complains the Doctor, 'I think she's cross with me for showing off,' he explains, patting the console apologetically. He checks some readings.

'It's no good,' he announces, 'There's a security field surrounding the space station. I can't materialize outside without setting off a dozen alarms but I can get through them and land inside unnoticed.'

A few moments later the TARDIS has materialized and you are ready to explore.

The Doctor wonders if you'd like to lead the way out of the TARDIS.

If you accept the offer, go to 29. If you prefer to follow Martha and the Doctor, go to 95.

The TARDIS materializes inside the space station. You hurry to the police box doors to explore but the Doctor calls you back.

'Hang on a minute, safety checks first,' he tells you.

Martha gives you a sympathetic smile. 'I know how you must be feeling. It's so exciting to step out into somewhere new but it's best to make sure that it's safe first.'

The Doctor is checking various readouts.

'Oxygen-rich atmosphere, gravity about 80 per cent of Earth normal, acceptable temperature range... I think I can call this one as "Safe to Explore."'

'So there's probably a gang of armed maniacs waiting for us outside,' murmurs Martha with a wink. 'What does the scanner show?' she asks.

The Doctor looks a bit sheepish. 'Not a lot actually. Shall we see for ourselves?'

If you go first, go to 29. If you let Martha and the Doctor go first, go to 96.

'Sorry, sorry, sorry,' you blurt out feeling totally embarrassed. You try and get yourself up and help Martha up at the same time but only succeed in losing your balance again as the TARDIS lurches violently, sending the pair of you to the floor.

'Doctor!' Martha complains, helping you to a handrail.

'Not a lot I can do about it,' he shouts out from the console, which is sparking and flashing alarmingly. He dances around it pulling at levers and pushing at switches in an attempt to regain control. Finally the TARDIS seems to respond and things begin to calm down.

'What was that?' asks Martha.

'I don't know — but it's down there.'

The Doctor points at the screen, which shows a space station orbiting a planet.

If the Doctor decides to take some more readings, go to 62. If the Doctor decides to materialize outside the space station, go to 83.

Before you can get too depressed about being left by the TARDIS, a powerful wind whips up and the TARDIS engine sounds fill the air and it rematerializes exactly where it was before.

'He's come back for me,' you whisper.

'He may have been away for months,' points out the Time Crocodile. 'Time machine, remember.'

Suddenly the doors open and the Doctor appears, full of energy and wild-eyed.

'It's about time,' he says ushering you inside. You begin to explain that he's only been gone a minute but he quickly hushes you.

'No, no, no... It's the time distortion. This Professor Morrow's trying to find a way to travel in time but if we can't shut down his experiment it's going to cause a massive rupture in space/time. I'm going to need you.'

If the TARDIS lands in the Control Centre, go to 10. If the TARDIS lands in the same spot, go to 12.

Inside you are delighted to find the Doctor. He's with a giant tortoise.

'Ah, there you are at last,' says the Doctor, 'I was wondering when you'd get here. This is Kyle,' adds the Doctor, indicating the talking tortoise.

'Kyle was helping Professor Morrow with his time experiment,' the Doctor explains.

'Until it all went pear-shaped and the Professor disappeared!' adds the tortoise in a depressed tone.

'It's the time experiment that's been causing all these time distortions. Like the one I fell through to get here,' the Doctor tells you, 'We need to stop the experiment before it ever gets started.'

Taking the tortoise with you to help with the task at hand, you return to the TARDIS and travel back in time.

If the TARDIS lands in the same spot as before, go to 31. If the TARDIS lands in the Control Centre, go to 89.

As the Professor reaches his hand out to launch the experiment, the Doctor activates a setting on the sonic screwdriver. The Time Crocodile and the tortoise clutch their heads and collapse in a heap. At the same moment you pull the power switch and shut it off.

'What are you doing?' screams the Professor, 'What's happening?'

'I'm sorry,' the Doctor tells the Professor, 'but I really do have to stop this right now.'

The Professor watches as the Doctor unlocks a glass case at the centre of the machine from which a glowing ball of light emerges. It shines with an intense warm light. The light washes over the prone figures of the crocodile and the tortoise and they disappear.

The glowing creature introduces itself. 'I am a traveller from beyond.'

'Beyond what?' you ask.

'Beyond your comprehension,' it tells you.

'Probably just the future then,' comments the Doctor with a wink.

'My presence here was a mistake. I will have to remove the relevant parts of memory from all these humans,' announces the alien. Immediately it passes through the Professor causing him to faint. The Doctor hurriedly steps in front of you and Martha.

'You can leave me to handle these two,' he tells it.

A golden tendril of light peels off from the main orb and enters the Doctor's forehead. Moments later it retreats.

'Very well Lord of Time,' it says after a moment, 'I thank you for my freedom.'

And then with another flash of multi-coloured lights it disappears.

'Right then,' says the Doctor looking at you, 'time to get you home I think.'

Back in the TARDIS the Doctor offers you the chance to launch your final TARDIS journey.

If you accept, go to 70. If you decline, go to 53.

When you get inside the Central Control room you find that it looks very much as you remember it, but here, in the recent past, it is full of activity. In the inner room the Professor is completing the final steps before initialising his time experiment. He dictates into a recording device.

'If I'm right this time-sensitive material will enable me to open up a time corridor, to another locale and time,' he records.

The Doctor makes for the door. 'I have to stop this now!'

'No,' insists another voice. It's the Time Crocodile in humanoid form — and he clearly wants to stop the Doctor from interfering. He points a weapon at the Doctor.

Seeing that the Time Crocodile is fully focused on the Doctor, Martha taps you on the shoulder and points to another door nearby.

If you escape without being noticed, go to 30. If you're spotted, go to 37.

'None of you move.'

It is the wild-eyed man in the white coat. He is unshaven and dishevelled.

'Professor Morrow, I presume,' the Doctor says in a friendly tone and holds his hand out to shake. 'I'm here to help you,' the Doctor insists.

The Professor waves his laser weapon in the direction of you and your companions.

'No one can help me,' he mutters, 'None of you.'

And then to your surprise he begins to cry.

'It's all gone wrong,' he explains, 'I don't know what to do. It's out of control.'

'If I can travel back in time to the point where the experiment started I can stop all this,' the Doctor tells him. 'Let me get back to my ship Professor and I can make it all better again.'

If you all go to the TARDIS, go to 33. If someone shoots the Professor, go to 38.

The Time Crocodile tells you to put the weapon down. 'That's not a toy,' he warns you and watches as you put it back where you found it.

'I don't understand,' you say, 'how did a zoo become a research centre?'

'It's not a zoo it's a fake zoo,' the crocodile explains. All the animals are robots. It's a recreation of an old-fashioned zoo. There was a real fad for this sort of thing in the early 24th century.'

'Trouble is,' continues the crocodile, 'fashion moved on. Suddenly the past was just too old-fashioned. Places like this were shutting down all over the known universe. The Professor picked this up cheap because he needed somewhere to set up his time experiments. Here we are.'

You've reached a door marked Control. You push at the door.

If you're with the Doctor, go to 34. If you're with Martha, go to 40.

The Doctor hurries in to the TARDIS. Everyone follows, including the Professor.

He is astounded. 'What is this place?' he mutters.

'This is a proper time and space machine,' you tell him.

The Doctor is running some kind of scan with his instruments. 'I need the access code to your computers,' he tells the Professor.

The Professor joins him and quickly types a password. 'Thank you,' says the Doctor as screen after screen of data begins to flash across his screens.

'Does that make any sense?' Martha asks him.

'I'm afraid it does,' he answers her.

He looks at you all gravely. 'There's a flux point in time and space near this planet. It's a weak spot in the real universe, a place where particles from the Time Vortex can leak into normal space time.'

If this makes sense, go to 22. If no one understands, go to 58.

'You may have your doubts about my work, but believe me I do have the animals' best interests at heart,' insists the Professor. 'Please come with me...'

The Doctor says nothing as the Professor leads you all through the zoo to his main lab.

'I'm under pressure to sell my discoveries.'

'Who from?' asks Martha.

'I'm not sure. The contact has all been through a corporation but I think that aliens might be behind it.'

'And what is it that they're so interested in?'

'I've created a creature that can move through time at will.'

'What?'

The Professor nods. 'To be honest I'm not quite sure how it happened. An accident in the DNA lab. I think.'

The Doctor doesn't look very convinced. 'I'm sure there's more to it than that.'

If you've met the Time Crocodile, go to 25. If you've not met the Time Crocodile, go to 59.

'Experiment Five'.

There is a click and the creature falls silent.

'That's quite enough from you,' says a new voice. 'Sorry, give them the power of speech and you can't shut them up!'

The speaker is a man in his forties, dressed in a white lab coat. 'I'm Professor Morrow,' he tells you.

The Doctor introduces you, Martha and himself.

'Are you the zoo keeper?' you ask him.

'Not exactly,' he confesses. 'I inherited this place but I no longer operate it as a zoo.'

'What do you operate it as then?' asks the Doctor and you can hear a slight edge in his voice.

'I use it as a lab. I'm a geneticist. A lot of these old Earth creatures are all but extinct. I'm trying to save them.'

If you are in the lab, go to 60. If you are in or by a cage, go to 93.

You step out of the TARDIS and find yourself in a brightly lit room that's clean and cold and full of machines that look vaguely medical. The Doctor and Martha are already looking around.

'This place reminds me of my teaching hospital,' Martha comments, picking up what looks like a set of surgical instruments.

The Doctor points to a large glass window, beyond which a room full of cages can be seen. 'Some kind of vet practice, perhaps?' he speculates.

You explore a little further. None of the cages appear to be occupied.

'Where is everyone?' you wonder.

'Perhaps there was some kind of contamination, a disease or something and they had to evacuate,' Martha wonders.

'Give the lady a prize!' a new voice interrupts, sarcastically, 'But you've got it wrong.'

If the speaker is a tortoise, go to 27. If the speaker is a crocodile, go to 61.

You step out of the TARDIS and find yourself in what appears to be an entrance hall with ticket booths and turnstiles.

'It's a zoo! Look,' exclaims Martha, who has been looking at a wall map.

'A space zoo?'

The Doctor nods. 'One of the less glorious exports from your home planet.'

Martha is surprised. 'But zoos do a lot of great conservation work. Captive breeding programmes keep endangered species alive.'

'Which wouldn't be necessary,' comments the Doctor, 'If you could just let animals be in their natural environments.'

Martha looks at you. 'Never forget he's an alien,' she mutters, nodding at the Doctor.

'I heard that!' says the Doctor, waving his sonic screwdriver at the nearest turnstile and walking through, ' Shall we take a look around?'

If you turn a corner and see a crocodile, go to 28. If you here a gruff voice saying 'Hello', go to 27.

You and Martha watch in amazement as the Doctor rushes around the central console flicking switches and pulling levers.

'Is there anything we can do?' you ask. 'Just stand back and admire my driving skills,' the Doctor tells you with a laugh. Just then the TARDIS rocks violently.

'Oh behave,' complains the Doctor, 'I think she's cross with me for showing off,' he explains, patting the console apologetically.

He checks some readings. 'We're in!' he announces with glee but then his face falls. 'These readings are worrying...'

'Radiation?' you ask.

'No,' the Doctor shakes his head, 'Raw time energy. Dangerous stuff.'

He considers for a moment and then tells you that he needs one of you to stay in the TARDIS to check the time distort reader.

You and Martha exchange a look.

If you suggest Martha should stay, go to 51.
If you volunteer to stay, go to 68.

'I think you're being a bit mean,' Martha says giving you a wink.

'Me? Mean?' the Doctor sounds incredulous.

'Would it really hurt to let our young friend here have just one trip?'

You look over at the Doctor trying to look keen without looking desperate. He looks you up and down.

'I don't take just anyone,' he tells you.

Martha stands up for you again.

'Come on — a kid from Earth — you know you can rely on one of those...'

The Doctor looks at you over his black-rimmed glasses. 'Can I?' he wonders out loud.

'Yes, of course you can,' you hear yourself saying. 'And I promise to do what I'm told!'

'Well of course,' says the Doctor, 'I'd expect nothing less...'

If you remember to say thank you to Martha, go to 69. If a warning light flashing on the console distracts you, go to 64.

Inside you are delighted to find the Doctor. He's with a giant tortoise.

'Ah, I was wondering when you'd get here,' says the Doctor.

'Who's this?' asks the tortoise in a nervous voice.

'Don't worry,' the Doctor tells him, 'they're with me. This is Kyle,' he adds, 'He was helping Professor Morrow with his time experiment,.

'Until it all went pear-shaped and the Professor disappeared!' adds the tortoise in a depressed tone.

'The time experiment that's been causing all the time distortions?' you ask.

'Just like the one I fell through to get here,' the Doctor agrees. 'We need to stop the experiment before it ever gets started.'

Taking the tortoise with you to help, you return to the TARDIS and travel back in time.

If the TARDIS lands in the same spot as before, go to 31. If the TARDIS lands in the Control Centre, go to 89.

The tortoise leads you along a corridor. He doesn't seem inclined to talk any more so you ask the Doctor why the zoo appears to be empty.

Suddenly an alarm sounds.

'Quickly, follow me,' cries the tortoise. But before you can do anything, a sliding security door drops from the ceiling, cutting off the section of corridor in which the tortoise and Martha are standing.

The Doctor grabs you by the hand and you run in the opposite direction. A second security door is descending but you both manage to scramble under it.

You reach a three-way crossroads and hesitate, not sure which way to go.

A wild-eyed and slightly manic man appears carrying a large evil-looking weapon. 'Stop or I'll shoot,' he orders you.

If the Doctor uses his sonic screwdriver to activate another security door, go to 74. If the Doctor pulls you into the nearest room, go to 13.

Sitting at a desk in an office chair is a slumped figure — the body of a man. The Doctor reaches out to place a hand on his shoulder but as soon as he does the body crumbles to dust.

'Was that... Professor Morrow?' you ask.

The Doctor nods. 'I'm afraid he paid the price for daring to experiment with time travel. We have to find the thing he's using to power this experiment. Whatever it is.'

You spot a map of the zoo and notice that something has been scribbled on it in red pen.

'Does this mean anything?'

The Doctor hurries over. 'Yes, I think it does. See here — the quarantine area. That's where he must be holding his time traveller.'

'Thank you, that's exactly what I needed to know!' says the Time Crocodile.

If he then laughs manically, go to 56. If he sounds genuinely grateful, go to 107.

'We shouldn't have trusted him,' you mutter.

'Who said we did?' replies the Doctor.

Before your eyes an amazing transformation is taking place. Like one of those toy robots that turns itself into a rocket, the Time Crocodile is transforming before your eyes. Its rear legs are lengthening and its front claws are turning into hands.

'It has multiple configurations, the crocodile look was just a disguise...' explains the Doctor.

'Do you mind not talking about me as if I'm not here?' demands the alien creature, now humanoid in shape and posture. It still has a reptilian scaly skin and the head of a crocodile.

'So who are you really?'

'I am TA4008, and I am here to stop this madness. And thanks to you I now know exactly what I need to do.'

If the Professor is dead, go to 21. If the Professor is alive, go to 20.

The Doctor adjusts his sonic screwdriver to a new setting and starts firing it at the area in which the Time Crocodile was last seen.

'If I can agitate any remaining time particles I might be able to reverse the transition,' he tells you as the Time Crocodile begins to take shape from thin air.

'What happened?' demands the Time Crocodile as he materializes fully.

'I did,' the Doctor tells him, 'You've got a nasty case of time spillage and I'm the Time Plumber!'

'I don't understand,' he whines. The Doctor explains to the Time Crocodile about the crack in space/time. 'Why don't I just show you?' he says, working the controls.

Moments later he opens the police box doors to reveal a view of space across which an ugly blue tear can be seen. It fizzes and bubbles with energy. 'That's what needs to be plugged?' asks the Time Crocodile.

'I'm afraid so,' nods the Doctor.

'Oh no, Doctor, there must be another way?' Martha complains.

'I don't understand,' you say.

'He wants the crocodile to sacrifice himself, don't you?' explains Martha angrily.

'The time energy the Time Crocodile has absorbed should negate the leak. Everything will go back to normal,' the Doctor tells you all.

'And what happens to me?' asks the Time Crocodile. The Doctor doesn't say anything.

'Okay then answer me this one. What happens if I don't do this?'

'The tear gets bigger and bigger, faster and faster until...'

'Bang?' you suggest. There is a pause before the Doctor nods.

'Then there really is no choice,' says the crocodile bravely.

Without another word the crocodile walks out the door. Instantly there is a massive explosion of light.

If the Time Crocodile disappears, go to 104.
If the Time Crocodile comes back, go to 111.

The atmosphere is rather grim as the Doctor pilots the TARDIS back to the zoo. Eventually you can bear it no more and you break the silence.

'What happened?' you ask.

'The energies cancelled themselves out,' the Doctor tells you. 'End of emergency.'

'And the Time Crocodile?'

'Is no more,' says Martha flatly.

The Doctor says nothing as the TARDIS engines fade away. He leads you all out into the space zoo. You are back at the crocodile enclosure, inside which is the familiar shape of...

'The Time Crocodile! He's alive!' Martha is delighted.

'Just plain crocodile now,' the Doctor explains, grinning. 'Everything's back to normal. You've got a second chance,' he tells the Professor. 'Don't mess it up.'

The Doctor announces that its time to go. Back inside the TARDIS he asks you to pull a lever.

If you accept, go to 70. If you decline, go to 53.

'Put your hands up,' calls a voice. You look over and see a wild-eyed man in a white lab coat pointing a space gun at you.

'Professor Morrow, we just want to help,' the Doctor tells him.

'You mean you want to steal my project. Are you from one of the Corporations? I thought I'd be safe out here, hidden away from populated space but I should have known it wouldn't last. Who do you work for? One of the alien conglomerates?'

He's beginning to babble madly.

'We don't want to take anything,' the Doctor tells him.

'Speak for yourself,' says the crocodile appearing suddenly in a doorway. This latest arrival is too much for the Professor in his paranoia and he faints, collapsing unconscious across his desk.

If you believe the crocodile to be a robot, go to 102. If you believe the crocodile to be organic, go to 56.

106 As you wander through the zoo, passing hippos, giraffes, penguins and all the usual creatures you would expect to see in a place like this, you find it hard to remember that you're on a barren moon, somewhere in deep space, four hundred years in the future.

You decide to ask the Time Crocodile about it but are shocked to realise that he is no longer with you.

You turn back and nearly walk into the Doctor. The Time Crocodile is with him.

'Look who I've found!' he says, proudly.

'Our friend here was just explaining to me that Professor Morrow will either be in his flat or in the lab,' the Doctor tells you.

When you reach the chosen door you open it and go in.

If you choose to go to the Control Room directly, go to 105. If you decide to check the flat first, go to 101.

107 The Time Crocodile is glowing and changing. 'I knew there was something odd about him,' you mutter.

'You don't say!' replies the Doctor.

Before your eyes an amazing transformation is taking place. Somehow the Time Crocodile's rear legs are growing, extending, lengthening. And at the same time his fore legs are changing into arms with hands.

'It's a shape-shifter...' explains the Doctor.

'Do you mind not talking about me as if I'm not here?' demands the alien creature, now humanoid in shape and posture. Despite the change it still has a reptilian scaly skin and the head of a crocodile.

'So who are you?'

'I'm Agent Trahlen, a Time Agent from the future and I am here to stop this madness. And, thanks to your intervention, I now know exactly what I need to do.

If the Professor is dead, go to 21. If the Professor is alive, go to 20.

The Doctor pushes you out of the way and then more laser fire destroys the security device.

'Get to your feet and make no sudden moves,' a voice orders you. It is the Time Crocodile — in his bipedal humanoid form. In his claw he holds a laser weapon.

'Release the time element and be careful with it!' he orders you, gesturing at a glowing ball set at the heart of the Professor's Time Experiment.

'Oh yes, you wouldn't want to drop that,' adds the Doctor, winking at you.

You reach into the apparatus and touch the globe, which is slightly warm and soft. It's held in a springy cradle but with a little pressure it pops out and into your hands.

Carefully you extract the globe from the heart of the equipment and stand up.

'Bring it to me,' orders the Time Crocodile.

'Please?' suggests the Doctor.

The crocodile ignores him.

You glance at the Doctor. Does he really want you to drop it? He winks at you again.

You take a deep breath and hope you've understood. As you approach the crocodile you deliberately trip and drop the globe.

'No!' screams the crocodile, dropping his weapon and leaping forward.

The globe flies through the air. For a moment it feels as if everything is happening in slow motion. The crocodile is diving like a goalkeeper to catch the globe but he's not going to make it.

The globe hits the floor. The room is filled with multi-coloured light, exploding like an indoor firework display.

For a moment you are blinded but slowly your sight returns. The lab is a scene of total destruction. The Time Crocodile has vanished.

'Are you all right?' a familiar voice asks you.

If it's Martha, go to 5. If it's the Doctor, go to 9.

You follow The Time Crocodile down an avenue of animal cages.

'I don't understand,' you say. 'How did a zoo become a research centre?'

'It's a long story,' the crocodile begins. 'This started out as a tourist attraction. A recreation of an old-fashioned zoo. There was a real fad for this sort of thing in the early 24th century, lots of different tourist attractions were based on recreating classic twentieth and twenty-first century favourites.'

'But where did the animals come from?'

'Genetically engineered clone life forms,' the crocodile continues. 'Custom built for the zoo. And that was the problem. It turned out that no one was interested in a mock-up of something from four hundred years ago. So we closed. Here we are.'

You've reached a door marked Control. You push at the door.

If you're with the Doctor, go to 34. If you're with Martha, go to 40.

You watch with apprehension as the Doctor lets the crocodile out of the cage.

'Thank you,' he says, politely.

'And now,' says the Doctor 'perhaps we can have some answers. For a start something tells me you're not an average zoo inhabitant, are you?'

'Ten out of ten for observation,' remarks the crocodile.

'How did you get to be a talking crocodile?' you ask, incredulously.

'Oh I'm far more than just a talking crocodile,' he boasts, mysteriously.

'Really?' asks the Doctor, 'In what way?'

'I can travel in time. That's why I'm the Time Crocodile. At least I am usually. It's a bit complicated to explain but—'

The crocodile never finishes his sentence as a blast of intense light goes off like a flashbulb! When you open your eyes one of your companions has disappeared!

If it is the Doctor, go to 78. If it is Martha, go to 48.

The Time Crocodile steps back into the TARDIS, now glowing with the same blue light as the tear in space.

'Thank you, Doctor,' he says.

'My pleasure,' the Doctor tells him 'May I know who it is that I've helped today?'

'I am Ophursis, a traveller from a distant time. An accident in the Time Vortex left me... injured; scattered into tiny fragments but I was able to survive in the DNA samples the Professor was developing.'

'And then in the zoo animals themselves?' Martha guesses.

'Exactly. I needed to find a way to re-enter the Vortex and you gave me that. Now I can go home...'

The ex-Time Crocodile's ship vanishes and the Doctor returns the Professor to the Zoo. After saying your goodbyes the Doctor offers you the chance to launch your final TARDIS journey.

If you accept, go to 70. If you decline, go to 53.

Step into a world of wonder and mystery with Sarah Jane and her gang in:

1. Invasion of the Bane
2. Revenge of the Slitheen
3. Eye of the Gorgon
4. Warriors of the Kudlak

And don't miss these other exciting adventures with the Doctor!

1. The Spaceship Graveyard
2. Alien Arena
3. The Time Crocodile
4. The Corinthian Project
5. The Crystal Snare
6. War of the Robots
7. Dark Planet
8. The Haunted Wagon Train
9. Lost Luggage
10. Second Skin
11. The Dragon King
12. The Horror of Howling Hill